eggsistential thoughts

by gudetama
the lazy egg

Penguin Workshop
An Imprint of Penguin Random House

Text by Max Bisantz & Francesco Sedita

PENGUIN WORKSHOP
Penguin Young Readers Group
An Imprint of Penguin Random House LLC

ISBN 9781524784287   10 9 8 7 6 5 4 3

meh.

ah, the darkness.

don't find me . . .

seriously,
I just can't.

it's mine . . .

gimme a beat.

my bacon blanket
is my BFF.

that's personal.

nothing
to see here.

let me go.

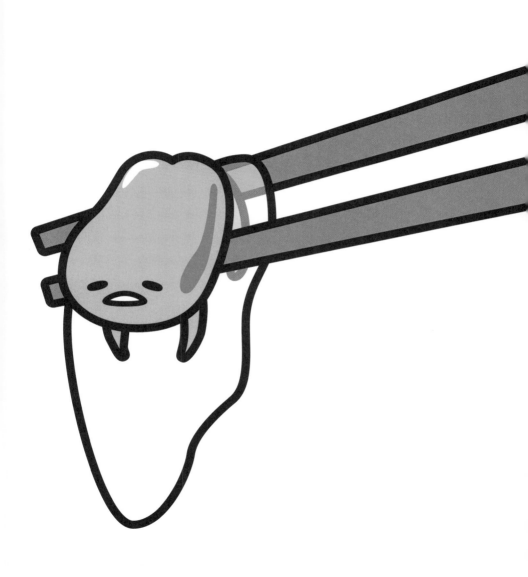

selfie . . .

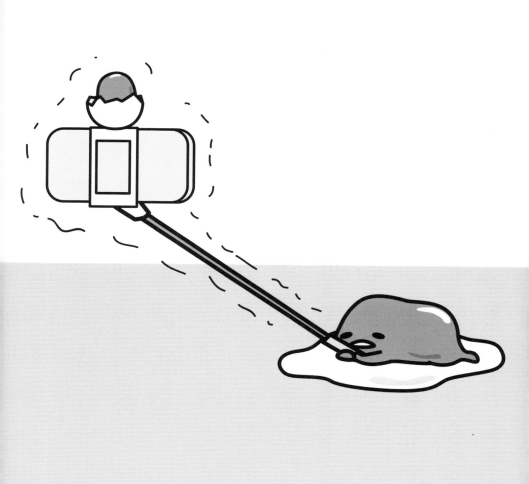

I'm feeling sluggish.

it won't be delivered in thirty minutes.

sleepy . . .

five more minutes.

eating is my
greatest desire.

I don't want to think about it.

argh...

no new followers.

first place
at being lazy.

lazy is
the new busy.

I just want to
be left alone.

can I go now?

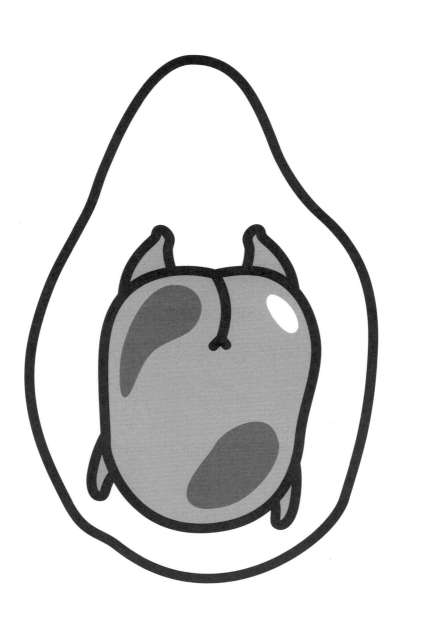